GOOD DA
BAD DAY

For Alison and Nick

Visit Catherine and Laurence Anholt's website at
www.anholt.co.uk

ORCHARD BOOKS
338 Euston Road, London NWI 3BH
Orchard Books Australia
Level 17-207 Kent Street, Sydney, NSW 2000

First published in 1990 by Orchard Books
This edition published in 2009

ISBN 978 I 40830 214 9

A CIP catalogue record for this book
is available from the British Library.

1 3 5 7 9 10 8 6 4 2
Printed in China

Orchard Books is a division of Hachette Children's Books,
an Hachette UK company.
www.hachette.co.uk

GOOD DAYS BAD DAYS

Catherine and Laurence Anholt

ORCHARD BOOKS

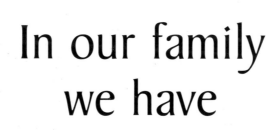

In our family
we have

good days

bad days

happy days

sad days

work days

play days

home days

away days

sunny days

snowy days

rainy days

blowy days

healthy days

sick days

slow days

quick days

school days

Sundays

dull days

fun days.

Every day's a different day

but the best day follows yesterday…

TODAY!